For Sophie, who showed me the way,
and for Amy, Ashey, and JoJo, for being
our destination. *JL*

For Sheila Barry and
Michael Solomon. Thank you for
believing in me. *SS*

Published in the UK in 2015 by Walker Books Ltd
87 Vauxhall Walk, London SE11 5HJ

First published in Canada and the USA as *Sidewalk Flowers* in 2015 by Groundwood Books

2 4 6 8 10 9 7 5 3 1

Copyright © 2015 JonArno Lawson
Illustrations © 2015 Sydney Smith

The right of JonArno Lawson and Sydney Smith to be identified as the author and illustrator of this work
has been asserted by them in accordance with the Copyright, Designs and Patents Act 1988

The illustrations were done in ink and watercolour, with digital editing.

Design by Michael Solomon

Printed and bound in Malaysia

British Library Cataloguing in Publication Data:
a catalogue record for this book is available from the British Library

ISBN 978-1-4063-6208-4

www.walker.co.uk

FSC
www.fsc.org
MIX
Paper from
responsible sources
FSC® C012700

Footpath Flowers

JonArno Lawson   Sydney Smith

WALKER BOOKS
AND SUBSIDIARIES
LONDON · BOSTON · SYDNEY · AUCKLAND